Littlebat's Halloween Story

WRITTEN BY **Diane Mayr**
ILLUSTRATED BY **Gideon Kendall**

Albert Whitman & Company
Morton Grove, Illinois

The sky was beginning to brighten with the red-orange glow of a spring dawn. Littlebat and his mother flew home to the library attic to roost.

PUBLIC
LIBRARY

All along the attic walls, bats took hold with their feet and clawed thumbs, wrapped their wings around their bodies, and settled down to sleep. Motherbat found a spot close to the attic floor. Littlebat took a long, deep breath and leaned against his mother. He closed his eyes…

Suddenly, Littlebat woke up.

Sounds of laughter were coming from a small hole. Carefully, he stuck his head through and peeked down. The room was full of children!

Then it became quiet. A woman began…

"A little girl with golden hair was walking through the woods…"

Littlebat was fascinated. He listened intently until the end.

"…and after that, the Three Bears never forgot to lock their door again!"

Sighing with pleasure, Littlebat crawled back to Motherbat and fell asleep.

That night, Littlebat said to his mother, "I saw people below. What do they do there?"

"They read," said Motherbat.

"Read?"

"Yes, they look in books and find stories."

"I heard one about the three bears," said Littlebat. "It was so good! I wish I'd been closer. I couldn't see the porridge."

"Littlebat," his mother said, "you must *never* get close enough for a look. It's dangerous!"

"I won't," said Littlebat with a sigh. "I'll just listen."

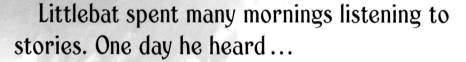

Littlebat spent many mornings listening to stories. One day he heard...

"A caterpillar was
eating, eating,
creeping, creeping,
spinning, spinning,
sleeping, sleeping."

"Ssh...," the woman whispered. Littlebat inched closer to hear...

"Many days and nights went by,
one morning, out came..."

"A BUTTERFLY!" the children shouted. The shout startled Littlebat. What was this butterfly that made the children yell so loud? He *had* to take a look. He leaned forward a little more...

And a little more . . .

He saw . . . a giant moth! A moth like those
he and Motherbat caught at night. Littlebat
became so excited he lost his grip and fell
into the room!

The children screamed and ran in circles.
The woman waved her book at Littlebat to
shoo him away.

He zoomed back up to the ceiling and scooted
through the hole.

"Mama, Mama!" he squeaked.

"What's the matter?" his mother asked.

Littlebat told her what had happened. "I was so frightened, Mama!"

"Oh, Littlebat, are you hurt?"

"No, Mama, I'm okay...but...but...I would like to see the pictures up close!"

"No!" said his mother.

"Never?" asked Littlebat.

Motherbat stared into the room below. "Well...maybe there's a time when it can be done," she said. "You must wait for changes."

"Changes?"

"You'll see."

Summer was coming! The nights grew shorter but the bats were busier. There were thousands of mosquitoes, moths, and mayflies to eat each night, before flying back to the attic.

The busy summer nights were tiring, but Littlebat always stayed awake for the stories.

One day, while he listened, he looked around the room. Changes!

He crawled up to where his mother slept and whispered, "Mama, is it time? Can I go now?"

His mother peeked through the hole. "Not yet, Littlebat. Keep looking."

That night there were changes all around.

But not the right ones.

Over the long, hot summer Littlebat listened
and watched. New decorations appeared. The
children wore shorts. And shoes without socks.
Whenever Littlebat saw something different,
he asked, "Mama, Mama, is it time?"
"Not yet, sweetie. Keep looking."

Summer came to an end. The air became
cooler, and in the weeks that followed, the
children started wearing jackets and sweaters.
Once again, the room changed.

"Mama?"

Motherbat looked. She saw apples. She saw
paper leaves of yellow, orange, and red. "Soon,
Littlebat, soon!" she said.

With the fall, the nights grew longer again. The bats were not as busy now. Each night there were fewer and fewer insects to catch.

In the early morning light, the leaves on the trees blazed red and gold. They were plucked by chilly breezes and tossed to the ground.

The bats were slowing down. It was nearly time for their winter's sleep. Littlebat still crawled to the hole for stories, but now he listened with his eyes closed. He was tired of looking for changes.

One day he heard his mother say, "Littlebat, look. It's time!"

Littlebat opened his eyes. He stretched and looked down into the room.

What he saw made his eyes open WIDE.

"Go quietly, Littlebat," Motherbat whispered. "Have fun!"

And he did.

To bats and crickets and all the little creatures
that share our spaces. — D. M.

I dedicate my first book to the memory of
my grandfather, Sidney Binder, and to all four
of my fantastic parents. — G. K.

Library of Congress Cataloging-in-Publication Data

Mayr, Diane.
Littlebat's Halloween story / by Diane Mayr ; illustrated by Gideon Kendall.
p. cm.
Summary: Littlebat loves to listen to the stories being told below the attic where he sleeps,
but he has to wait until just the right time to get close enough to see the pictures.
ISBN 0-8075-7629-8 (hardcover)
[1. Bats — Fiction. 2. Libraries — Fiction.] I. Kendall, Gideon,
ill. II. Title. PZ7.M47375 Li 2001 [E] — dc21 2001000801

Text copyright © 2001 by Diane Mayr.
Illustrations copyright © 2001 by Gideon Kendall.
Published in 2001 by Albert Whitman & Company,
6340 Oakton Street, Morton Grove, Illinois 60053.
Published simultaneously in Canada by General Publishing, Limited, Toronto.
Printed in the United States of America.
10 9 8 7 6 5 4 3 2

The display and text typeface is Blackfriar.
The design is by Scott Piehl.

For more information about Albert Whitman & Company,
visit our web site at www.awhitmanco.com.